A. Watt

THE
MERRY
CHRISTMAS
ACTIVITY BOOK

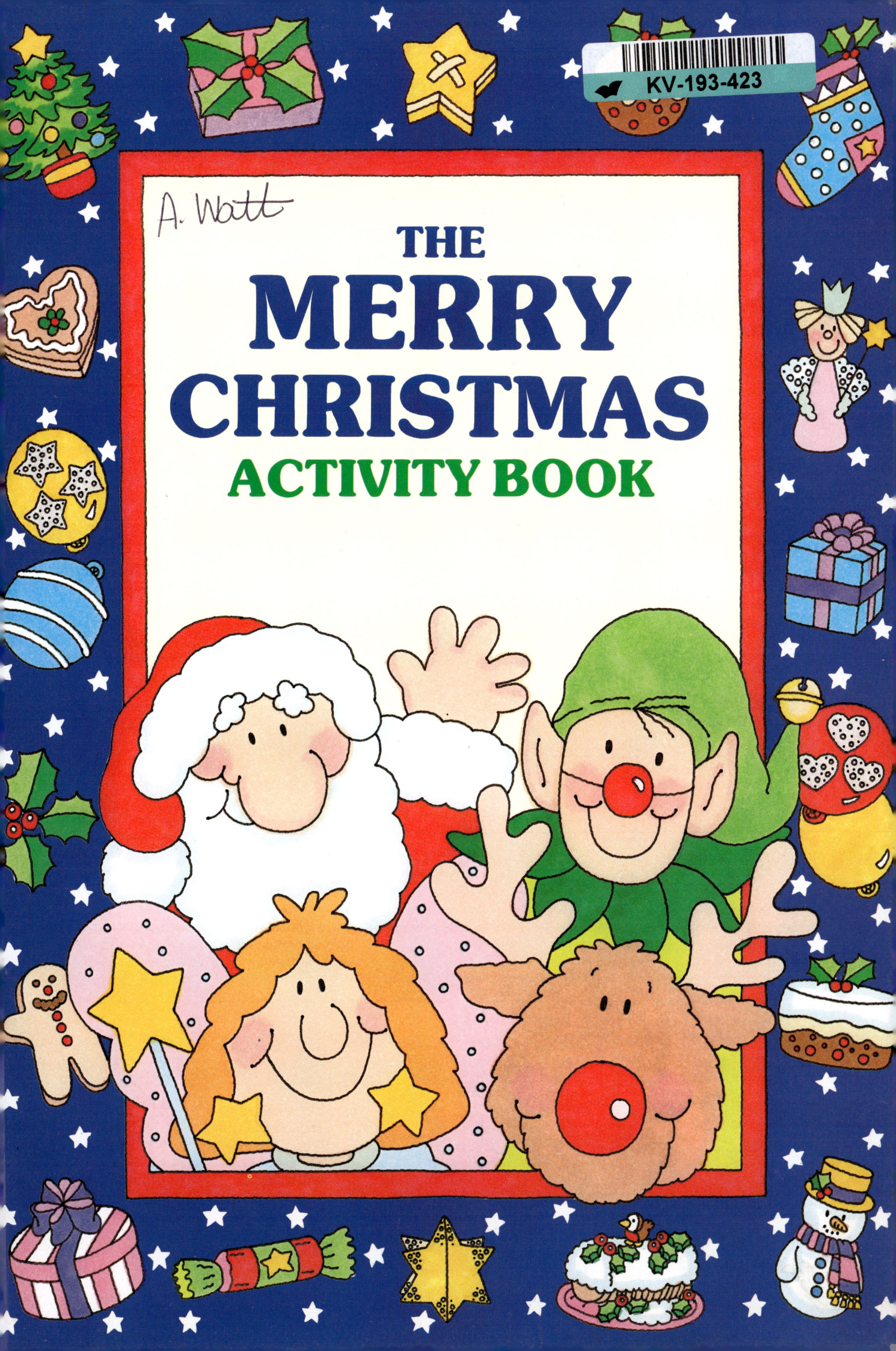

Invites and Christmas Cards

If you're having a party, the first thing you need to do is make sure you have some guests. Try some of these fabulous invite ideas and no guest will be able to resist.

Don't forget to add your name, address, phone number and the date, time and theme of your party.

You can use these ideas to make special Christmas cards too.

• You will need •

- stencils
- felt-tip pens
- scissors
- thin card
- glue/glue pen
- glitter
- coloured felt
- stuffing
- needle and thread
- ribbon and braid
- net fabric and cellophane
- sweets
- cocktail sticks
- biscuit cutters

✦ Glittery invites ✦

① Write a message and stencil shapes on a piece of card. Trace over what you have drawn with a glue pen.

② Sprinkle with glitter. Shake surplus glitter onto a piece of paper.

③ You will have a glittery message. Or make stencil shapes from card, glue glitter on one side and write your message on the back.

✦ Gingerbread hearts ✦

① Stencil a heart shape onto paper. Cut it out. This is your pattern.

② Cut two hearts out of ginger-brown felt.

③ STUFFING
Sew the two hearts together leaving a gap at the top. Stuff with a little padding and sew up the hole.

④ Decorate with white braid and some felt holly. Sew a label to the heart and write on your party details.

ADD YOUR GUEST'S NAME IN FELT

⑤ You could make Christmas pudding and snowball invites in the same way.

✦ Stocking card ✦

① Copy this stocking shape onto a folded piece of card.

② Cut along the dotted line.

③ Glue along the inside edge and stick together.

④ Decorate with stencils and trim with cotton wool. Pop a tiny card and some chocolate money in the top.

⑤ Make a hole and thread a ribbon through to hang your card up.

☆ Holly leaf invites ☆

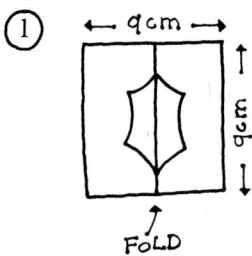

① Stencil a holly leaf onto a piece of green paper.

② Fold the paper in half and cut out the leaf.

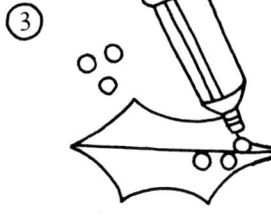

③ Cut out two or three red holly berries and glue them to the leaf.

④ Write the party details in tiny writing on the back.

☆ Edible gingerbread invites ☆

Use the gingerbread recipe on page 9. Make the dough and roll it out to 4mm thick.

① Cut with a 12cm wide biscuit cutter.

② Make two holes with a cocktail stick and bake.

③ Write your invite on a piece of paper or a label 10cm × 8cm.

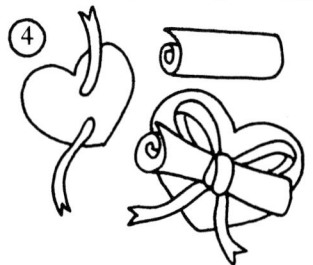

④ Thread ribbon through the holes, roll up the invite and tie to the heart.

☆ 3D Christmas cards ☆

Use your stencils to draw shapes of snowmen, trees, stars etc.

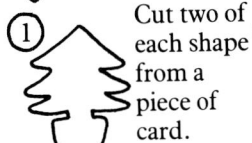

① Cut two of each shape from a piece of card.

② Colour and decorate them brightly on both sides with coloured pens, paper and glitter.

③ Fold both shapes in half.

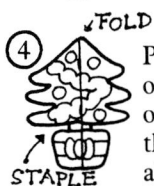

④ Place one shape on top of the other and staple them together along the fold.

⑤ Open it out and you have a 3D card. You could write your message on one side or all four.

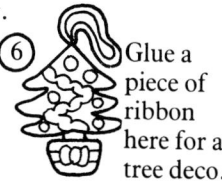

⑥ Glue a piece of ribbon here for a tree deco.

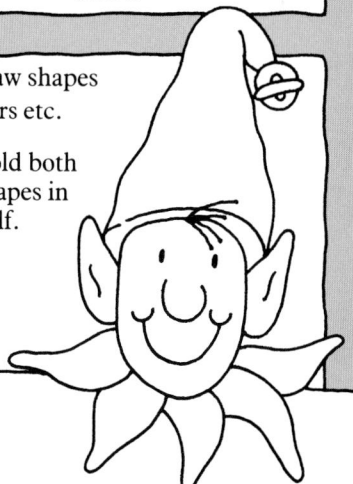

☆ Bookmark card ☆

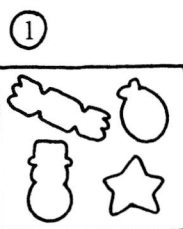

① Choose a stencil shape such as the snowman.

② Draw the shape onto a piece of card.

③ Colour him in and draw on a smiley face and some coal buttons. Cut him out.

④ Cut a flap from the back of the card like this. Write on your message.

CUT HERE

HAPPY CHRISTMAS

Don't throw your cards away after Christmas. Save them to make gift tags. Cut out the part of the card you want to use, make a hole, thread it with ribbon or cotton and attach it to your pressie.

☆ 3

Fancy Dress Costumes

Fancy dress Christmas parties can be brilliant fun. Try to find old trousers, T-shirts, sweatshirts and tights in red, green and brown to make up the ideas on these two pages. You might need some help.

Then why not think up some costume ideas of your own?

Have a good look around jumble sales for lots of different fabrics – sheets, blankets, clothes etc.

They can be transformed into really wonderful costumes.

Buttons, zips, lace and trimmings can also be cut from old clothes.

Give everything a good wash before you use it though!

- **You will need**
- stencils
- large pieces of green/red fabric (old sheets or curtains will do)
- fabric paint and dye
- assorted ribbons, buttons, bells, belts, elastic and velcro
- crêpe paper
- white and brown furry fabric
- cotton wool
- coloured felt
- wadding
- a hula hoop
- a balaclava
- wellies, plimsolls
- pillow case

☆ Santa Suit ☆

① Sew white furry fabric or glue cotton wool to the cuffs and along the edges and hem of a red shirt, sweatshirt or old dressing gown. Do the same to some trousers.

② ←60cm→ Cut a semi-circle of red fabric. Fold it into a cone shape and sew along the seam. Trim with white furry fabric. Make a pom-pom by gathering a square of furry fabric, stuffing it with cotton wool and securing with a few stitches. Sew it onto the point of Santa's hat.

③ Make a beard from a sheet of cotton wool or white furry fabric. Attach elastic to each side. Make cotton wool eyebrows and tape them carefully on top of your own.

④ Add a wide belt and a pair of wellies. Trim an old pillowcase with red ribbon to use for Santa's sack.

Masked balls are great fun!

☆ Reindeer ☆

① 15cm / 20cm

② 5cm / 10cm

③ 25 cm / 25cm

④ velcro

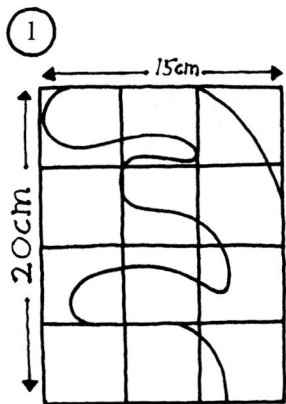

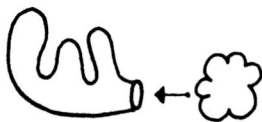

Follow this pattern to make a pair of antlers. Cut 4 out of grey felt and sew them together in pairs.
Leave the bottom edge open and stuff with wadding.

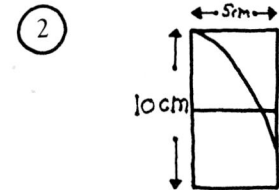

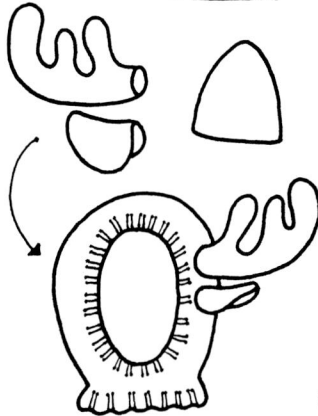

Follow this pattern to make a pair of ears. Cut 2 out of brown felt. Fold in half and sew to a brown balaclava together with the antlers.

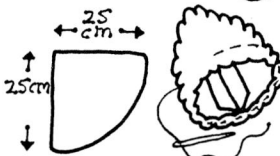

Sew very wide black satin ribbon round the cuffs of a brown jumper and the hems of a pair of trousers. Make a tail from brown furry fabric, using the pattern above. Sew it onto the back of the trousers.

Make a belt from wide yellow ribbon and trim it with bells.
Pop on a pair of black plimsolls and a red nose.

☆ Christmas Tree ☆

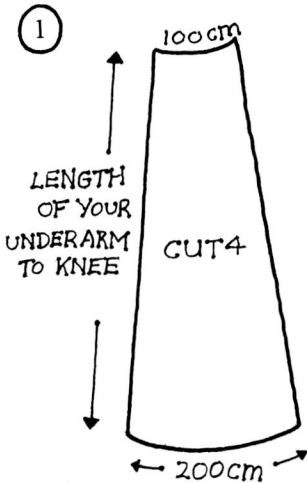

① 100cm / LENGTH OF YOUR UNDERARM TO KNEE / CUT 4 / 200cm

② hula hoop

③

④ 40cm / HAT

Wear an old green jumper, brown trousers and a pair of wellies.
Following the pattern above, cut 4 pieces out of green fabric, to make the main skirt of the tree. Sew together along the side seams.

Cut long strips of crêpe paper 14cm deep. Fringe one edge of each strip with scissors. Tack the crêpe paper around the green skirt until it is completely covered. Thread elastic through the top of the skirt and sew a hula hoop into the hem.

Make tree baubles and decos by stencilling various shapes onto thick card. Colour them brightly with paint and glitter. Stick them all over the skirt.

To make the hat, cover a green card cone with green crêpe paper fringes and attach elastic. Glue on cardboard baubles and decos and pop a star on the top!

How about a Fancy hat party?

5

Christmas Parties

Here are a few ideas for some finishing touches to make your party extra special. You can adapt these ideas to fit the theme of your party.

Invites

Make sure the envelopes are the right size for your invites and send them out in plenty of time. If you are having a theme party, make sure your invites are in keeping.

Fun flags

① Stencil shapes onto coloured paper. Cut them out and attach them to cocktail sticks. Write sandwich fillings on the front.

② Use biscuit cutters to make bread shapes then sandwich them together.

JAM HAM CHEESE

You will need

- stencils
- pencils
- felt-tip pens
- scissors
- coloured paper
- cocktail sticks
- glue
- sticky tape
- paint
- newspapers
- drawing pins
- thin card

Place markers

① Draw two circles onto white and brown card. Cut the top half of the white circle as above.

② Cut out two dish shapes like this in white card. On one dish cut from point A to point B.

③ Decorate with holly and stick all the pieces together as shown above. Slot the plates together.

④ Make a flag and write your guest's name on it – tape it to the back of the place marker.

LILY

Wall hangings

Bright wall-hangings can make a room look fab!
Put down lots of newspaper first.
Measure your walls from floor to ceiling and cut lengths of strong lining paper.
Paint on lots of splodgy shapes to match the theme of the party.
Hang up the pictures with masking tape.

Table decorations

① Decorate paper tablecloths with stencil shapes and crayons. You could even stencil on fabric using fabric crayons.

② Stencil and colour shapes onto paper cups and plates.

③ Self-adhesive gold and silver stars look lovely stuck on plastic glasses.

Home made toffees + biscuits wrapped in cellophane and tied with ribbons make great take-home pressies!

Party Themes

Hold a Christmas party with a difference. You could give a colour party, on a theme of gold, or black and white, or red, pink and white.

For a real change at Christmas, why not hold a tropical party, or a space, underwater, or spooky party?

This page will give you a few ideas.

Space party

Draw moon and star invites with your stencils. Sprinkle with glitter on one side and write details on the other. You could also draw planet and rocket shaped invites.

Cover the party table in crumpled silver foil. Stick on gold stars. Use foil containers to hold all the food and give your guests silver foil plates. Stick stars onto plastic glasses. Cut sandwiches with star-shaped cutters.

Cover balloons in glittery shapes and stripes to look like planets. Glue stars and sequins onto white and blue net fabric. Twist the net to make garlands and pin them to the ceiling. Stencil star and moon shapes onto card. Cut them out and cover them with glitter. Attach a piece of blue thread and hang them from the ceiling.

You and your guests can dress up as astronauts, star people, planets and even rockets.

Tropical party

Make invites like these using bright coloured paper. Cut 2 of each shape. Glue along the top edge to make a card and write a message inside.

Glue brightly coloured paper fish, starfish, shells and seaweed onto a blue paper tablecloth. Serve nuts, crisps and sweets in coconut and scallop shells. Make place mats from coloured paper shaped like watermelons.

Glue fish, starfish and shell shapes onto balloons. Paint bright wall hangings with splodgy shell, fish, wave and seaweed shapes. Make tissue paper flowers. Glue them onto green net fabric. Twist the net to make garlands and pin to the ceiling.

Dress up in loud shirts and bermuda shorts or maybe flower garlands and hula skirts.

Tissue paper flowers

String flowers onto lengths of thread to make garlands for your guests.

1. Cut lots of brightly coloured tissue paper into rectangles.

2. Roll each one up, scrunching together one side as you go.

3. Secure the base of the flower with a stapler or sticky tape.

4. Cut out leaves from green tissue and attach to the flower heads.

Tree Deco's

The tree is probably the most important of all Christmas decorations. Dressing the tree is very exciting. On the next two pages there are some ideas for tree and other decorations for you to make yourself that won't cost a fortune.

When you start to decorate your tree always put the lights on first starting at the top and working your way down. Next, drape tinsel, streamers, ribbon etc. in big loops around the tree. Load the tree with all your decorations, the more the merrier. Finally, pop a fairy, angel or star on the top of the tree and make a wish!

If the pot your tree is in looks a bit ugly, tie a skirt of brightly coloured crêpe, foil or wrapping paper around it. Add a big bow in another bright colour.

If you're going to use the cooker, let an adult know what you're doing.

← Popcorn festoons

Christmas star

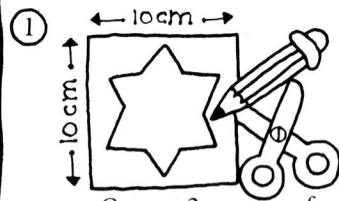

① ← 10 cm →
10 cm
Cut out 2 squares of card. Cover each side with a different colour foil. Cut each square into a star shape.

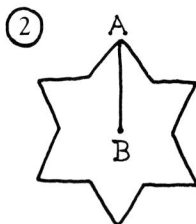

② A B
Draw a line from A to B. Cut along this line on both stars.

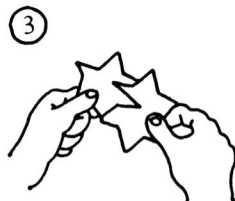

③ Slot the two stars together. Use sticky tape to hold the points in place.

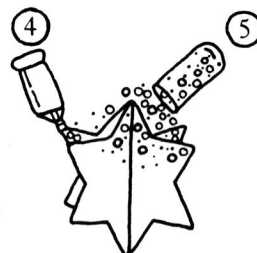

④ Dab some glue onto the points and sprinkle with glitter to make your star sparkle.

⑤ Attach a piece of green garden wire to one point. You may need help to tie your star to the top of the tree.

Christmas fairy

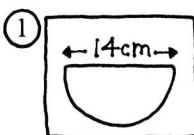

① ← 14 cm →
Cut out a semi-circle of silver foil. Fold into a cone and tape.

② Cut a triangle from a doily and stick it to the back of the cone for wings.

③ Draw a face onto a ping pong ball. Use wool for the hair and make a tiny crown out of silver paper.

④ Carefully skewer the ping pong ball onto a cocktail stick. Push the stick into the cone. Tape a pink pipe cleaner to the back and bend it round for the arms.

It's a good idea to buy a live tree which you can plant in the garden after Christmas, and use again year after year.

Indoors, make sure your tree is planted in a stable pot of damp soil or sand.

Keep it happy with plenty of water but stand the pot in a large saucer to protect your floor when the water drains through.

8

Pastry tree decos

To make dough:
- 4 cups of plain flour
- 1 cup of salt
- 2 tablespoons of vegetable oil
- water
- paints
- ribbon
- varnish
- biscuit cutters

1 Put the flour and salt into a bowl. Add the oil and the water. Knead on a floured board.

2 Roll out the dough to 4mm thick. Cut out shapes with biscuit cutters. Place on a well-floured baking tray. Make a hole in each shape.

3 Bake for one hour at 250°F/120°C/gas mark 3. When the pastry has cooled paint the shapes and varnish.

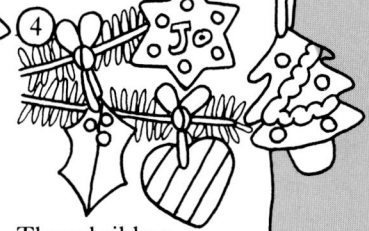

4 Thread ribbon through the holes and hang the shapes on your tree. Don't eat them!

Gingerbread tree decos

- 225g plain flour
- 110g sugar
- 110g butter
- 2 teaspoons of ginger
- 75g golden syrup
- 1 beaten egg

To finish off:
- water
- icing sugar
- biscuit cutters

1 Blend everything together to make a dough. Roll out the dough to 4mm. Cut out shapes with biscuit cutters.

2 Place the shapes on a lined baking sheet. Make holes in each shape. Bake for 15 minutes at 350°F/180°C/gas mark 4.

3 Mix a little water and icing sugar. When the biscuits are cool, pipe on icing sugar patterns.

4 Thread ribbons through the holes. Pop a few biscuits in a decorated box for a fab pressie!

Fortune cookie tree decos

For the cookies:
- 80g golden syrup
- 60g caster sugar
- 60g butter

To finish off:
- paper
- pencils
- 20cm lengths of ribbon

1 Melt cookie ingredients in a saucepan. Place teaspoons of mixture on a lined baking sheet and bake for 10 minutes at 140°F/170°C/gas mark 3.

2 The jumper granny knitted will not fit. You will meet Father Christmas. Write messages and fortunes on small pieces of paper 2cm × 6cm.

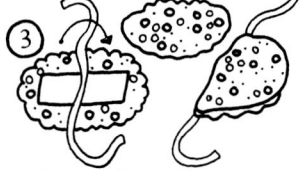

3 Leave the cookies to cool briefly. Place your messages and ribbons in the centres and fold the cookies over.

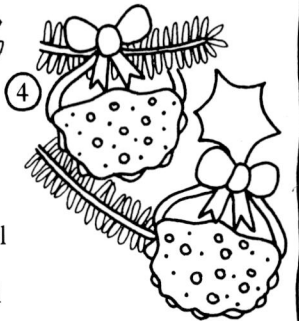

4 Tie your cookies onto the tree.

Mini Christmas pressies

- card
- pencils
- scissors
- glue
- wrapping paper
- ribbon
- ruler

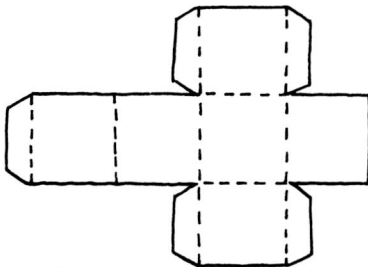

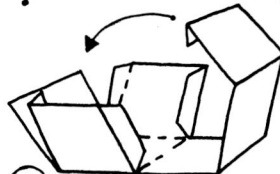

1 Copy this shape onto thin card. Use a pencil and ruler. Cut it out. Fold along the dotted lines and glue the sides together (see above).

2 Put small gifts and sweets inside the box and wrap it in attractive paper. Tie it up with ribbons and bows. Pop it on the tree.

Popcorn festoons

Using a needle, carefully thread lots and lots of popcorn onto very long, strong cotton. Tie a knot at each end so the popcorn won't pop off!

Christmas Decos

Christmas garlands

Materials:
- Coloured tissue paper
- pencil
- scissors
- glue stick
- stiff card
- string

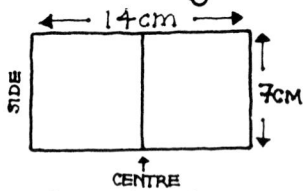

1. Cut out lots of rectangles this size from different coloured tissue paper.
   - 14cm
   - 7cm
   - SIDE
   - CENTRE

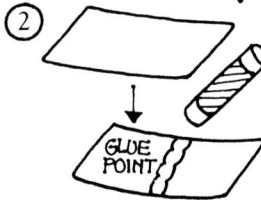

2. Glue the rectangles together down the centre line.
   - GLUE POINT

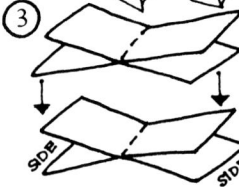

3. Glue the pairs of tissue together down both sides.
   - SIDE

4. Make your garland as long as you like and then glue a piece of stiff card and some string to each end.
   - END

Holly garlands

Materials:
- green tissue paper
- red card
- pencil
- scissors
- glue stick
- stiff card
- thick thread

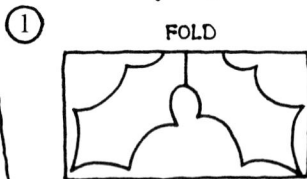

1. Stencil holly shapes like this onto folded rectangles of green tissue paper.
   - FOLD

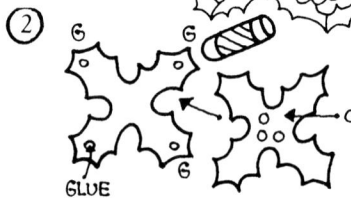

2. Glue leaves together in pairs and stick red paper holly berries on both sides.
   - GLUE

3. Glue the pairs of leaves together. Glue circles of looped red card to each end to hang up your garland.
   - GLUE
   - LOOPED CARD
   - 4CM DIAM

Sweet garlands

Materials:
- thick ribbon
- wrapped sweets
- stick-on stars
- scissors
- stencils
- thick card
- stapler
- sticky tape
- curtain rings
- needle and thread

1. Cut one length of ribbon 140cm long and 3 short lengths 110cm long. Tie the short ribbons into bows. Sew or tape one at each end and one onto the centre of the long piece of ribbon.

2. Decorate the ribbons with stencilled shapes.

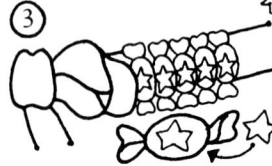

3. Stick silver and gold stars onto wrapped sweets and attach them along the top of the ribbon with sticky tape or staples.

4. Sew curtain rings onto the back of the ribbon behind each bow to hang the garland.

Christmas crackers

Materials:
- crêpe paper
- tissue paper
- stiff paper
- cracker snappers
- card tubes
- cotton thread
- ribbon
- small gifts
- paper hats
- small decos
- jokes on small paper squares

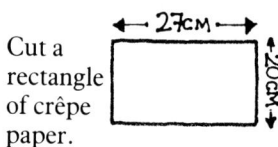

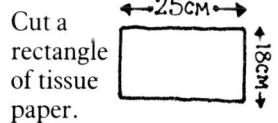

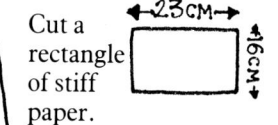

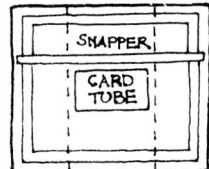

1. Cut a rectangle of crêpe paper.
   - 27CM
   - 20CM

   Cut a rectangle of tissue paper.
   - 25CM
   - 18CM

   Cut a rectangle of stiff paper.
   - 23CM
   - 16CM

2. Layer the pieces of paper like this. Put the tube and snapper in the centre. Roll the papers around the tube and secure with glue or tape.
   - SNAPPER
   - CARD TUBE

3. Tie one end with thread. Drop in a gift, hat and joke. Tie the other end.

4. Tie ribbons at each end of the cracker and zigzag the edges with scissors. Decorate with stars, drawings, lace, guests names etc.
   - ROB

YOU COULD MAKE SOME MINI CRACKERS TO HANG ON THE TREE!

Balloons

- balloons
- felt/fabric pens
- scissors
- glue
- scraps of wool
- stick-on stars and shapes
- small sweets

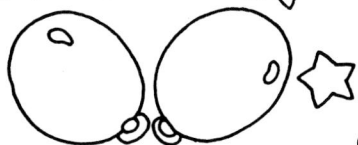

You could make funny face balloons to look like your guests! Tie them to chair backs and see if your friends know where to sit! Glue on felt eyes, a nose, a mouth – even some big pink ears! Add wool or cotton wool for hair.

Jazz up balloons with stick-on stars and shapes. Push in small sweets, like Smarties, before you blow them up. Apart from looking fab and rattling nicely it's great fun popping them to get at the sweets!

Glitter balloons

- stencils
- balloons
- pencil
- scissors
- glue stick
- thin foam
- corrugated card
- cork
- paper glue
- glitter

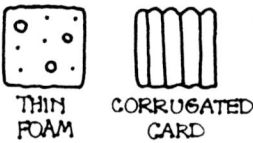

THIN FOAM

CORRUGATED CARD

① Cut one square of thin foam and one of corrugated card. Glue them together.

② Stencil one of your shapes onto the square and cut it out. Glue a cork onto the back of the card.

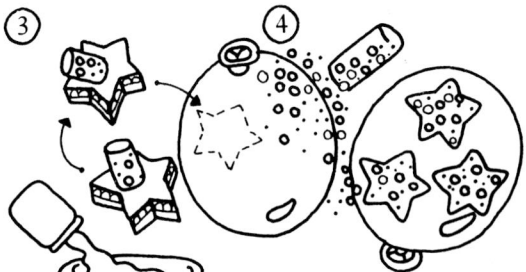

③ Dip this stamp into a saucer of paper glue and press it onto a blown up balloon.

④ Sprinkle the balloon with glitter. Shake off any extra and leave it to dry. Make lots of different stamps and a roomful of balloons.

Clove orange

- an orange
- ribbon
- pins (Mind your fingers!)
- lots of cloves

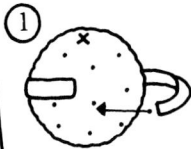

① Wrap a piece of ribbon around an orange and pin it carefully in place.

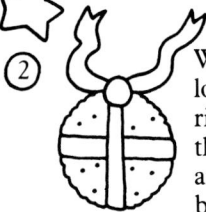

② Wrap a very long piece of ribbon round the other way and tie a tight bow.

③ Cover the orange by pressing cloves into the skin.

Apple candles and snazzy candles

- one large Granny Smith apple
- apple corer
- candles
- coloured ribbon
- tiny pins
- gold tape
- stick-on stars
- scissors

APPLE CORER

Core the apple so it is wide enough to put the candle in. Press the candle into the hole – easy!

PIN

☆ Cut lengths of ribbon a little longer than the candle. Turn one end of ribbon under and pin it to the top of the candle. Pull the ribbon carefully to the bottom and pin. Do this 2 or 3 times for a stripy effect.

Try sticking stars and hoops of gold tape around candles too.

11

Party Games

Start off with some of these games, and you'll soon have a great party atmosphere.

Make sure you prepare the games before everyone arrives. Enjoy yourselves!

The Chocolate Game

- a huge bar of chocolate
- a knife
- a fork
- a pair of gloves
- a scarf
- a hat
- a coat
- wellies
- dice
- a sweet tooth!

☆ Sit in a circle on the floor, place the chocolate, knife and fork and all the clothes in the middle.

☆ Take it in turns to throw the dice. Whoever throws a six leaps into the middle, quickly puts on all the clothes and begins to eat the chocolate with the knife and fork.

☆ As soon as another player throws a six it is their turn to leap into the middle, put the clothes on and eat as much of the chocolate as they can before the next six is thrown.
The game finishes when all the chocolate is eaten!

Fish for Gold

- stencils
- pencil
- scissors
- thin, coloured card
- metal paperclips
- dowelling
- string
- magnets
- a large bucket

☆ Using your stencils draw 20 Christmas trees and 20 hearts onto coloured card and a star onto gold card. Cut them out. Attach a metal paperclip to each shape, and place them all in a bucket.

☆ Make a magnet rod for each player. Tie a 35cm length of string to one end of a 30cm piece of dowelling. Tie a magnet to the end of each piece of string.

☆ Everyone fishes for gold until the bucket is empty. Score 5 points for each Christmas tree, 10 points for each heart, and 25 points for the gold star!

12

☆ Egyptian Mummies ☆

- a timer
- miles and miles of loo roll
- a judge
- a degree in Egyptology!

☆ Divide players into pairs. Give each pair a roll of soft loo paper.

☆ Set the timer for two minutes. At the word "GO" players should wrap their partners from head to toe in paper!
(Be careful not to cover the nose and mouth – you don't want smothered Mummies!)

☆ The best wrapped Mummy is the winner!

☆ Who am I ? ☆

- pencils
- strips of paper 2cm × 8cm
- sticky tape
- a sense of humour!

DARTH VADER

☆ Send players out of the room one by one, whilst the rest of you decide which famous person or character they will be.

☆ Once you have decided on a character, write his or her name down on a piece of paper and call the player back into the room.

☆ Stick the name to the player's forehead with a little sticky tape. Don't let them see who they are!

☆ When each player has been named, take it in turns to ask questions to find out who you are. The first one to guess correctly is the winner.

☆ Santa's Sacks ☆

I won!

- 10 carrier bags/Santa sacks
- objects to smell, taste or touch

for example:
- orange peel
- a clove of garlic
- a sprig of mint
- a raw potato
- wet bread
- curry powder
- a tea bag
- parmesan cheese
- a sponge
- pepper

☆ Fill 10 carrier bags (Santa's sacks) with various different things for players to touch, taste and sniff.

☆ Number each bag from 1 to 10, and keep a record of the contents.

☆ Blindfold players and allow them, in turn, to guess what's in the sacks.

☆ The winner is the one who guesses the most contents correctly.

Small gifts – chocolate money, sugar mice, comics, balloons and even plastic ducks – make great prizes!

Christmas Pressie's

Everybody loves a homemade pressie!

A little time and thought makes a present very special, and the ideas on these two pages are cheap to make too.

Look for the symbols in each box to check who would like which present.

Mum • Granny • Aunty

Dad • Grandad • Uncle

Brothers • Cousins • Friends

Sisters • Cousins • Friends

• You will need •

- thin card
- glue
- scissors
- stencils
- pencils
- pens
- stars
- glitter
- lace

☆ Trinket boxes ☆

Brightly decorated boxes filled with home-made toffee, gingerbread and small gifts make fab pressies.

See page 9 for instructions to make boxes like these.

Draw on and colour in stencil shapes. Decorate with stick-on stars or lace and ribbons. Add name tags.

Wrap toffee and gingerbread into large squares of net fabric or coloured cellophane.

Gather up the corners, tie with ribbon.

☆ Molly's toffee ☆

- 500g brown sugar
- ¼ pint of water
- 100g butter
- 100g golden syrup
- a small tin of condensed milk

- Let an adult know what you are doing

①

Grease a shallow baking tin and put it to one side.

②

Put all the ingredients into a saucepan. Stir over a moderate heat until the sugar has dissolved. Gently boil, stirring occasionally, for 15 mins.

③

Pour toffee into the tin. Remove when cold and break it into pieces. Wrap each piece in a square of greaseproof paper. Decorate each one with a gold star.

This is my mum's recipe for toffee!

deeelicious!

14

☆ Earrings and brooches ☆

- modelling dough (see page 9)
- biscuit cutters
- shells, buttons, sequins, pasta shapes etc.
- paint
- varnish
- strong glue
- earring clips
- safety pins

1. Roll out the dough to 4mm thick. Cut out shapes with biscuit cutters or a sharp knife.

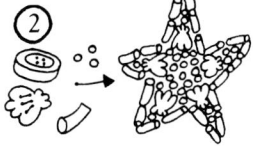

2. Press buttons, pasta, sequins etc. into the pastry shapes. Leave a few plain to paint later. Bake slowly for one hour at 250°F/120°C/ gas mark 3.

3. When the shapes have cooked, paint and varnish them. Shell brooches look nice just varnished.

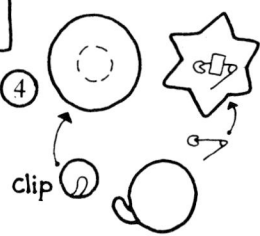

4. Glue clips, available from haberdashers, to the backs of earrings. Tape safety pins to the backs of brooches.

clip

☆ Jam jar snowscene ☆

- jam jar with tight screw-on lid
- small plastic decos
- waterproof glue
- small bottle of glycerine
- water
- glitter

1. Squeeze a little glue onto the base of the decos and stick them to the bottom of the jar. Leave them to dry.

2. Pour in the contents of the glycerine bottle and top up carefully with water. Replace the lid tightly and shake gently to mix.

3. Unscrew the lid and pour in some glitter. Screw the lid back on tightly. Shake the jar and you have a snow scene.

☆ Cress and mustard haircut cards ☆

- Very thick blotting paper
- waterproof ink pen
- pencils
- waterproof glue
- cress and mustard seeds
- saucer
- water

1. Draw a face in waterproof ink onto blotting paper and colour it in.

2. Draw lightly in pencil the areas where you would like hair to grow.

3. Lightly glue these areas and stick down your seeds. When the glue is dry the card is ready to send.

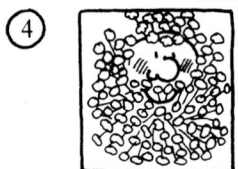

4. Tell your friends to keep the card in a warm place and moisten it with water. It will soon need a haircut!

☆ Spinning snake ☆

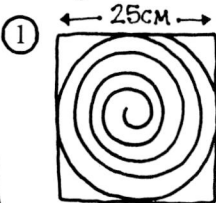

- thin card
- pens
- pencils
- scissors
- piece of string
- sticky tape

1. ←25cm→ Draw a circle onto a piece of card. Draw a spiral snake in the circle.

2. Now colour your snake with jazzy spots and stripes. Give it a pair of eyes and a mouth.

3. Cut along the outlines carefully and open it out.

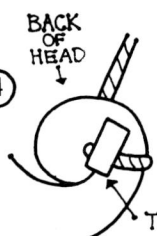

4. BACK OF HEAD. TAPE. Attach a length of thread through the centre of the head and secure it at the back with sticky tape.

5. When the snake hangs over a radiator it will spin round and round as the hot air rises.

radiator →

Christmas Wrapping

Presents can look so much more exciting if you take extra time to wrap them up. Why not have a go at making your own wrapping paper, crackers or fancy decorations? You can disguise a pressie too, as a post box, a Christmas tree or even a Christmas pud!

Try the suggestions on these two pages, then see if you can think up some ideas of your own.

• You will need •

- pens and pencils
- stencils
- scissors
- glue
- sticky tape
- thin card
- coloured card and paper
- crêpe paper
- white paper
- wrapping paper
- ribbon
- thread
- glitter
- corks
- flower pots

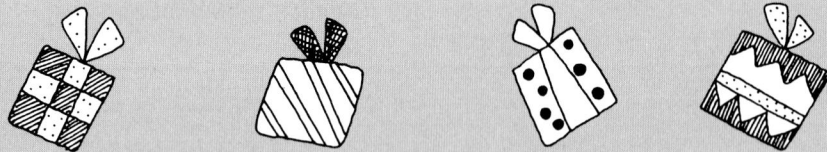

Wrapping

Stencil shapes onto large sheets of plain paper and decorate with pens, pencils and stick-on stars.

Tie your parcels with huge bows and streamers. You could even stick on wrapped sweets.

Glitter wrapping

① See page 11 to make these stamps

② Use paper glue to stamp shapes onto plain paper. Sprinkle with glitter. Shake off any extra glitter and leave to dry.

③ Wrap your pressie and tie a huge bow around the parcel.
Stick stencilled and glittered shapes onto the tips of the bow.
Make glittery gift tags too.

Holly box

① A   B

② CENTRE FOLD

③

④

⑤

Wrap your pressie in bright paper or silver foil. Measure your parcel from A to B.

Fold a piece of paper in half. Draw a holly leaf along the fold on both sides. Make its middle as long as A to B.

Trace four holly leaves onto green card. Cut them out and make a fold down the centre.

Make holly berries by glueing a small ball of cotton wool inside 2 sheets of red tissue. Twist the ends and snip them off when the glue is dry.

Glue the leaves and berries onto your parcel.

WRAP PRESSIES WITH BROWN PAPER + TIE WITH BRIGHT RED OR TARTAN RIBBON. SECURE WITH RED SEALING WAX. CHEAP + VERY CHEERFUL!

☆ Snowy post box ☆

Good for disguising bottles, tubes and cylindrical pressies.

① Cut a rectangle of thin red card to fit round your pressie. Secure it with sticky tape.

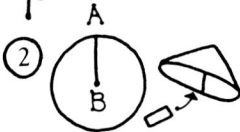

② For the roof cut a circle of red card a little bigger than the end of your tube. Cut a line from A to B. Make a cone and secure it with tape inside.

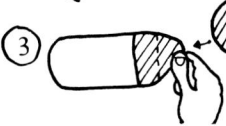

③ Cut a rectangle of black card to wrap around the tube. Tape it on. Fold the ends under to hold the pressie in. Stick a circle of black card over the folds.

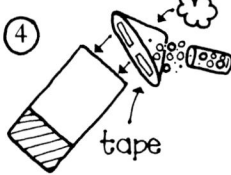

④ Tape the roof on with some folded tape. Stick cotton wool on the outside and add dabs of glitter.

⑤ Glue on a small black rectangle for the mouth of the postbox and a white rectangle for the gift label.

☆ christmas pudding ☆

Good for disguising anything round from ping pong balls to footballs!

① TRIM WITH SCISSORS

Place the pressie in the centre of a large square of giftwrap. The edges of the paper should just meet at the top of your pressie. Trim off the corners to form a circle of paper.

② Gradually pull all the sides up to the top and stick with tape. Pleat neatly all the way round and stick a paper circle on top.

③ Next, the icing. Cut out a large circle of contrasting paper. Trim the edge of the circle so that it is wobbly. Stick it on top of the pudding.

④ Stick sprigs of holly on top of the icing (see holly box instructions) and place the pudding on a foil plate.

☆ Christmas tree ☆

Good for disguising bubble bath, posters, smarties and other cylindrical pressies.

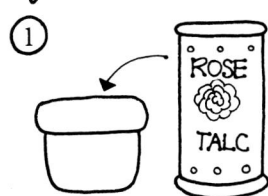

① Find a plastic flower pot just big enough to take the base of your pressie.

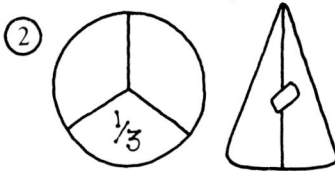

② Make a deep cone from 1/3 of a large circle of card. The cone should be 7cm shorter than your pressie. Cover the cone with bright green giftwrap.

③ Pop your pressie into the flowerpot and put the cone on top. Stick glittery shapes all over the tree and a blob of tinsel at the top.

☆ Christmas cracker ☆

Good for disguising practically anything!

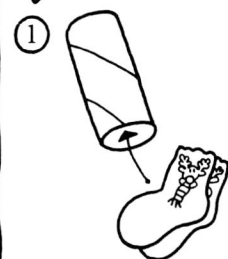

① Pop your pressie inside a cardboard tube.

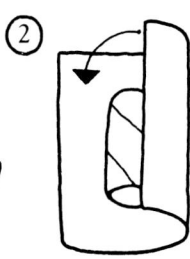

② Wrap the tube in a piece of crêpe paper.

③ Twist the paper at each end and tie with a ribbon.

④ Glue on Christmassy shapes. Add a gift tag.

Wow! what's in that one?!

Open your presents carefully to save the paper. You could use it to cover a school book. Save boxes for storage or use the card to make all sorts of other things.